Any Way You Slice It

For Maya and Rachel, Katie's fans
from the start!—NK

For the girls on Spring Street—J&W

Text copyright © 2003 by Nancy Krulik. Illustrations copyright © 2003
by John & Wendy. All rights reserved. Published by Grosset & Dunlap,
a division of Penguin Young Readers Group, 345 Hudson Street,
New York, NY, 10014. GROSSET & DUNLAP is a trademark of
Penguin Random House LLC.
Manufactured in China

Library of Congress Cataloging-in-Publication Data is available.

10 9 8 7 6 5 4 3 2 1

Proprietary ISBN 978-1-101-95133-0
Part of Boxed Set, ISBN 978-1-101-95128-6

Any Way You Slice It

by Nancy Krulik • illustrated by John & Wendy

Grosset & Dunlap

Chapter 1

"Watch out, Suzanne!" Katie Carew warned her best friend Suzanne Lock as the girls walked through the Cherrydale Mall. "You're about to bump into the jewelry stand!" The girls were allowed to walk around the mall alone, as long as they stayed close to the bookstore where Katie's mother worked. It was one of the best parts of having a mom who worked at the mall.

Suzanne moved to her left. "Thanks, Katie," she answered. "That was a close one."

"I don't know about this walking-backward thing," Katie said. "It's pretty dangerous. You could get hurt."

"Well, I can't stop now," Suzanne told her. "I've already been walking backward for forty-five minutes."

"How much longer until you break the record?"

Suzanne looked at her watch. "Only seventy-two hours and twenty-three minutes."

Just then, Jeremy Fox, Katie's other best friend, ran up to the girls. "Hurry up, Katie," he said. "We've got to get to Louie's Pizza Shop. He's about to make another pizza!"

Katie's face lit up. She loved watching Louie throw the dough in the air. He made a real show of it, twirling around and singing Italian songs. "Suzanne, can you run backward?" Katie asked.

"I can try," Suzanne replied.

Jeremy rolled his eyes. "Why don't you give it up?" he asked Suzanne. "You'll never break the record."

"How do you know?" Suzanne demanded.

"Well, you didn't break the seesawing

record, or the holding-your-breath record, or the hopping-on-one-foot record, did you?" he asked. "You've been trying to break a record all week!"

Suzanne frowned. "This is different!" she insisted. "Isn't it, Katie?"

Katie didn't answer. She hated it when her two best friends put her in the middle of one of their arguments. Besides, she didn't really know what to say. Suzanne had been trying all week to get into the book of world records. So far, she hadn't even come close.

Still, Katie knew Suzanne wasn't going to give up—at least not until she became interested in something else.

"Come on," Jeremy urged again. "I want to get a good seat, right near the pizza oven. Louie's is going to be mobbed. You know what it's like there on Saturdays."

Katie looked at Suzanne.

"You go ahead," Suzanne told Katie.

"Are you sure?"

"Yeah. Just save me a seat."

Katie smiled. "Thanks, Suzanne, you're the best!" she shouted as she ran off with Jeremy.

Katie and Jeremy didn't get very far before they heard a loud crash. The kids turned around and saw Suzanne sitting on the floor, covered in a mountain of women's hats.

"Suzanne banged into the Hat Rack!" Jeremy began to laugh.

But Katie didn't think it was funny. Neither did the manager of the Hat Rack clothing stall.

"Watch where you're going!" the manager shouted at Suzanne.

"I'm sorry," Suzanne said, blushing. "I was trying to break a record."

"Well, you almost broke my stall," the manager scolded. "Now get out of here, before I call security."

Suzanne jumped to her feet and ran . . . frontward.

"So much for the book of world records," Jeremy said to her.

"Don't you worry." Suzanne shook her head. "I'll find another record to break."

Chapter 2

Louie's Pizza Shop was very crowded by the time Katie, Jeremy, and Suzanne arrived. Lots of people liked to watch Louie make his pizzas.

Katie loved everything about Louie's Pizza Shop. She loved the jukebox in the corner. She loved the Italian ice and spumoni counter. She loved the smell of warm pizza coming out of the oven. But most of all she loved Louie. He looked just like a pizza chef should, with his big white shirt, long apron, and dark, twirly moustache.

"Hey, Katie Kazoo, over here!" somebody called out.

There was only one person in the world who called her Katie Kazoo—her friend George Brennan. Katie quickly spotted George and his best pal, Kevin Camilleri. The boys were sitting at a big table with Kevin's older brother, Ian.

"Where have you been?" George asked as Katie, Suzanne, and Jeremy sat down. "You were supposed to be here ten minutes ago."

"Shhh. Louie's just about to do a double twist," Ian interrupted excitedly.

Katie turned to look at Louie. The pizza chef tossed the big circle of dough in the air. Then he spun around twice, reached his hands out, and caught the pizza just before it hit the counter.

"All right!" Jeremy cheered.

"Louie, you rock!" Ian shouted.

"That pie's going to be pepperoni," George told the others. "And I'm getting a slice!"

Katie was a vegetarian. She'd been hoping

that Louie's next pie would be a spinach pizza. *Oh well.* She could wait. Katie couldn't go home from the mall until her mother got off work.

Louie ladled the sauce onto the pizza. His arm moved swiftly, leaving red sauce all over the dough. Next, he tossed some cheese into the air. The white mozzarella bits fell like snow from the sky. Then Louie took a few steps back and started flinging pepperoni slices at the pizza.

The pepperoni looked like little Frisbees as they flew through the air and landed on top of the cheese. Then, as he sang loudly, he added a pinch of his secret herbs. Finally, he slid the finished pizza into the oven.

The crowd cheered.

Louie took a bow and picked up another ball of dough. "Now for a Louie's veggie special!" he announced, smiling at Katie.

Just then, Becky Stern came running into Louie's Pizza Shop.

"Where have you been?" Suzanne asked her. "Louie already made a pepperoni pie."

"I'm sorry I'm late," Becky apologized in her soft Southern accent. "My mother wanted to stop and get a slice of pizza." She grabbed a chair and sat down next to Jeremy.

"Why didn't she get the pizza here?" Katie asked her.

"Yeah," Jeremy agreed. "Louie makes the greatest pizza in the whole world."

Becky smiled at him. "I believe you, Jeremy. After all, you do have the best taste!"

Jeremy blushed.

"But my mother had a coupon for a free slice at Olives and Oregano," Becky continued.

"Olives and Oregano is on the other side of town," Katie said, raising her eyebrows. "Why did you go all the way over there?"

Becky shook her head. "There's a new Olives and Oregano right here in the Cherrydale Mall. It's next to the Flower

Power flower shop. Today is the Grand Opening. They're giving out all sorts of free food."

"Did you say free food?" a woman at the next booth asked Becky.

Becky nodded. "Free pizza and soda. I just had some."

The woman stood up. She grabbed her little girl by the hand. "Come on, Alexandra," she said. "Let's try the new restaurant."

Then a terrible thing happened.

Something that had never happened before.

Louie dropped the pizza dough.

"Sorry, folks," Louie said, as he scooped up the dirty dough from the floor, changed his rubber cooking gloves, and picked up a new ball of dough. "Let's try that again."

Louie tossed the new ball of pizza dough in the air. He spun around in a circle as it flew through the air, and sang an Italian song. But he wasn't smiling the way he usually did when he was making pizza.

Louie was obviously upset. And Katie was pretty sure it didn't have anything to do with the fallen pizza dough.

Chapter 3

"Boy, does Becky have a crush on you!" Suzanne teased as she, Jeremy, and Katie climbed into the backseat of Mrs. Carew's car later that afternoon.

"She does not!" Jeremy protested.

"Does too," Suzanne answered back. She batted her eyes and imitated Becky's accent. "Oooh, Jeremy. You have the best taste!"

Jeremy blushed. He pushed his glasses up on his nose. "I wish Becky had never moved here!" he exclaimed suddenly.

Katie gulped. "Jeremy, don't make wishes like that," she warned.

Katie knew all about making wishes.

Sometimes they came true—and that could lead to big problems.

It had all started one really bad day at school. Katie had lost the football game for her team, ruined her favorite jeans, and burped in front of the whole class.

That night, Katie had wished that she could be anyone but herself. There must have been a shooting star flying overhead or something when she made that wish, because, the very next day, the magic wind came.

The magic wind was a wild storm that seemed to blow only around Katie. It was really powerful. So powerful, in fact, that the magic wind was able to turn Katie into somebody else.

The first time the magic wind came, it changed Katie into Speedy, the class hamster. Another time it turned her into her own dog, Pepper.

But the magic wind didn't turn Katie only into animals. Sometimes it turned her into grown-ups, like Lucille the school-lunch lady, and Mr. Kane, the principal of her school, Cherrydale Elementary School.

The magic wind had also turned Katie into other kids, like Becky or Jeremy. Being some-body else could be really tough. When she was Jeremy, Katie didn't even know whether to use the girls' room or the boys' room!

"Don't worry, Jeremy," Suzanne said,

interrupting Katie's thoughts. "Becky will get over you . . . as soon as she gets some brains."

"Okay, why don't you three talk about something else?" Mrs. Carew suggested quickly. "And don't forget to buckle up," she added as she prepared to pull out of the parking lot.

Chapter 4

The next afternoon, Katie arrived at the mall with her mother at exactly 12:00. "Hurry up, Mom!" she cried out. "It's lunchtime. I want to make sure I get a seat at Louie's."

Katie's mom laughed. "You certainly like pizza," she said.

"It's not just the pizza. It's fun at Louie's. Everyone from school is there—except Mrs. Derkman of course. And that makes it even more fun."

Mrs. Derkman was Katie's very strict third-grade teacher. She was also Katie's next-door neighbor. Ever since a few months ago, when Mrs. Derkman had moved into the house beside Katie's, it seemed like Katie saw her everywhere—in school, on the street, even at barbecues in Katie's own yard. But she never saw Mrs. Derkman at Louie's. Mrs. Derkman was not a big pizza eater.

"All right, Katie," Mrs. Carew said, as her daughter pulled her toward Louie's. "I'm going as fast as I can."

But when Katie and her mother arrived at Louie's Pizza Shop, there were plenty of seats left. In fact, there were only three people in the restaurant—a father and his two sons.

"Slow day, Louie?" Mrs. Carew asked as she sat down at a table near the pizza oven.

Louie pounded hard on a pile of dough. "It's only slow here," he answered sadly. "It's mobbed at Olives and Oregano."

Mrs. Carew nodded understandingly. "It's a new restaurant. People will get tired of it."

Louie shook his head. "I don't think so. Olives and Oregano is part of a big chain of restaurants. They have lots of money to spend on advertising." Louie reached under the counter and pulled out a newspaper. "Look at this."

Katie and her mother looked at the newspaper. There was a full-page ad:

"They have clowns and a magician performing all day," Louie told Katie and her mom.

"Big deal," Katie said. "Nobody puts on a better show than you, Louie. Or has better pizza."

Louie smiled at her. "Thanks, Katie," he told her. "I wish there were more kids like you."

"Don't worry, Louie," Mrs. Carew said. "Things will pick up. It's still early."

Sure enough, someone else walked into the restaurant. "Katie!" Suzanne shouted. "Here you are." She held out a wooden paddle with a red rubber ball attached to it with a rubber band. She was hitting the ball with the paddle. "Thirty-eight. Thirty-nine. Forty," she counted as she tapped the ball.

"I told you I'd meet you here," Katie told her.

Suzanne nodded. "Forty-one. Forty-two. Forty-three."

"What are you doing?" Katie asked her.

"I'm trying to break the world paddleball record. Fifty. Fifty-one."

"When did you start that?" Katie asked her.

"A few minutes ago," Suzanne replied, still

counting. "They were giving out the paddles at Olives and Oregano."

Bam! Louie pounded the dough so hard, the counter shook. The noise broke Suzanne's concentration. She missed the ball.

"Drat," she said. "Now I'll have to start all over."

Katie put her hand on the paddle. "Not now."

"But I'm going to break the record," Suzanne insisted.

"You can do that later," Katie assured her. She knew Louie didn't want to see an Olives and Oregano paddle bouncing up and down in his restaurant. "Let's sit down and get a slice. Mandy and Miriam should be here any minute. They always have lunch at Louie's on Sunday."

"I don't think they're coming today," Suzanne said. "I just saw them eating hoagies at Olives and Oregano."

Louie didn't say anything. But judging by the frown on his face, Katie could tell he'd heard everything Suzanne had just said.

Olives and Oregano was taking over the food business in the mall.

This was so not good.

Chapter 5

After they'd finished their pizza, Suzanne and Katie took a walk around the mall. They stopped in Bead It!, the bead store near the BookNook. They tried on blue eye shadow at the Beauty Barn, and checked out jewelry at the Golden Earring stall.

"Katie, are you ever going to get your ears pierced?" Suzanne asked. Suzanne had her ears pierced in first grade. Katie, on the other hand, was still wearing clip-on earrings.

"It doesn't hurt," Suzanne assured her. "At least not a lot."

Katie shrugged. "Let's go to the flower shop," she suggested.

But it was almost impossible to get to the Flower Power flower shop. The area around the store was filled with crowds of people hanging around outside Olives and Oregano. Clowns were giving balloons to the kids who walked by, and pretty girls in Italian folk-dancing costumes were handing out free food coupons to adults.

"Hey, Katie Kazoo!" George cried out from a seat near the front of the restaurant. He was sitting at a table with Zoe Canter and Manny Gonzalez.

"What are you doing here?" Katie asked her classmates. "Why weren't you at Louie's? He's been making pizzas all afternoon."

Manny shrugged. "They're giving out free soda here!"

"Come on, sit down," Zoe said to Katie and Suzanne. "We've got room."

Suzanne plopped down in a chair near Zoe. But Katie didn't move. She didn't want to eat at a restaurant that was giving Louie so much trouble.

"I don't think so," she said. "I've got to get back to my mom's store."

"Oh, you can stay for a little while," Manny said. "We just ordered some fries. You can share."

"Yeah," George said. "We're getting tons of food. My mom gave me money and told me to stay here until she gets back from returning things at the jeans store."

"Come on, Katie, sit down," Suzanne urged. "Your mom isn't going home for at least an hour. And, besides, they have chocolate milk shakes on the menu."

Katie loved chocolate milk shakes.

"Do you know how they get milk shakes?" George asked.

"How?" Katie asked him.

"From nervous cows!" George laughed at his own joke.

Katie laughed, too. "Okay, I'll stay," she said finally. "But only for a minute. And I'm not going to eat anything."

Suzanne shrugged. "Okay, but I'm ordering a shake."

Katie sat down and looked around the restaurant. On the wall, there were huge paintings of Italian olive groves. All of the waiters and waitresses were dressed in red, white, and green uniforms, which matched the colors on the big Italian flag that hung over the door. And, of course, there were plenty of olives and oregano on all the tables.

Katie sighed. Compared to Olives and Oregano, Louie's Pizza Shop didn't look like much. But Louie's pizza was the best. Katie was sure of that.

"Aachoo!" Suddenly, George put his hand to his nose as he sneezed. As he pulled his hand away, there was a big, green glob in his fingers.

"Eeew!" Suzanne exclaimed.

Katie was pretty grossed out, too—until she realized that the green glob was actually an olive.

"Gotcha!" George laughed.

Katie began to relax. She loved being with her friends, especially on the weekends. She reached into the olive bowl and pulled out a thick, salty black olive. Yum.

But as she popped the olive in her mouth, Katie got a sick feeling in her stomach. At that very moment, Louie passed by the window of Olives and Oregano.

Louie didn't wave or smile. He just kept on walking with a sad look on his face.

Katie was sure Louie had seen her and her friends sitting at the table. She knew his feelings must be really hurt.

"I'm a terrible friend," she muttered sadly to herself.

Chapter 6

Katie didn't go to the mall for a whole week after Louie spotted her in Olives and Oregano. She was too embarrassed. But when Saturday came around, her mother told her she had to go.

"I have to work all day, and your dad is out of town on a business trip," Mrs. Carew explained. "I need you to spend the day at the mall. There's nowhere else you can go today."

Katie was not about to face Louie alone. She made sure that all of her friends would be there with her. At 12:00, Katie, Suzanne, George, Jeremy, Kevin, Becky, Miriam, Mandy, Zoe, and Manny all met outside Louie's Pizza Shop.

There was a new sign in the window. It said:

GOING OUT OF BUSINESS

Katie couldn't believe her eyes. It just wasn't possible. Louie's Pizza Shop had been in the Cherrydale Mall ever since Katie could remember. Suddenly, she forgot all about being embarrassed. She had to talk to Louie!

"Louie, you aren't really going out of business, are you?" Katie asked as she raced into the pizza shop.

Louie nodded. "I am," he told her.

"But why?" Katie asked.

"I'm losing all my customers to Olives and Oregano," Louie explained. "They advertise on TV and in newspapers. I can't afford to do that. And if I can't advertise, I can't get people to eat here instead of there."

The kids all looked at each other. They felt bad about eating at Olives and Oregano.

"Don't be sad," Louie said. "It's okay. I'm going to move to Florida. My sister has a place there, and she says retirement is really very nice." Louie tried to smile, but Katie could tell he was sad about leaving.

POP!

Suddenly, a loud noise came from where Suzanne was standing. Her face was covered with a huge wad of pink bubble gum.

"Sorry," Suzanne apologized. "I'm trying to break the biggest bubble-gum bubble record." She struggled to pull globs of bubble gum from her chin, cheeks, and nose. "What are you all laughing at?" she demanded as her friends giggled.

"Too bad you can't break a record, Louie," Jeremy said, turning his attention away from Suzanne.

"What kind of record?" Louie asked.

"I don't know," Jeremy said, "the most customers in a pizza shop or something."

"That would be nice," Louie agreed.

Suddenly, a big grin came over Katie's face. "Jeremy! You're a genius!" she exclaimed.

"Of course he is," Becky said, with a smile. "Everyone knows that."

Jeremy blushed and moved away from Becky. "What are you talking about?" he asked Katie. "Louie, I know how you can get free advertising in newspapers and on TV," Katie told him.

Louie looked at her curiously. "How?"

"All you have to do is get newspaper reporters to write articles about your restaurant," Katie said.

"They wouldn't want to do that."

"They would if you were going to have a big pizza-eating contest," Katie explained. "Who can eat the most pizza in Cherrydale. That would be big news."

Louie looked at Katie. "You sure have big ideas for such a little girl." He laughed, as he pulled out a pencil and paper. "Any thoughts on how we can let people know about the contest?"

"Well, I could put an article about it in the *Class 3A Times*," Jeremy suggested. Jeremy was editor of the class newspaper.

"And my daddy could post a sign about it on the bulletin board at his office," Becky added.

"I'll bet my mom would put a sign in the window at the BookNook," Katie volunteered.

"And we could hand out flyers for you here in the mall," Suzanne suggested, as she chomped on a new wad of gum.

"I guess that takes care of everything," Louie said.

"Then you'll do it?" Katie asked hopefully.

Louie scribbled some numbers on his pad of paper. "Well, if I charge ten dollars a person to enter the contest, and five dollars a person to watch the contest, I might be able to afford it."

"Great!" Katie said. "Then you won't have to move to Florida."

Louie sighed. "Well . . . " he said slowly, "let's just wait and see."

Chapter 7

"Hey, Katie Kazoo! My mom said I could enter Louie's pizza-eating contest!" George announced in the school yard early Monday morning.

Katie smiled. "I knew you'd be the first to sign up. No one likes to eat as much as you do, George."

Just then, Kevin strolled onto the playground. "Guess what?" he asked the others. "I'm entering the pizza-eating contest. I can't wait to sink my teeth into Louie's yummy tomato sauce!" Kevin was wild about tomatoes.

George stared at Kevin. "What do you

mean, *you're* entering the contest? *I'm* entering the contest."

"So?" Kevin said. "We can both enter . . . of course *I* will win."

"Don't be so sure, Kev," Jeremy said. "You know what a big eater George is."

"Oh, please," Suzanne butted in, suddenly. "Kevin is already the tomato-eating champ of Cherrydale Elementary. He'll definitely win."

Suzanne would say anything just to disagree with Jeremy.

"I don't think so," Jeremy remarked.

And Jeremy would say anything just to disagree with Suzanne.

"Kevin, I know you'll win," Suzanne said firmly. "Especially because

I'm going to help you! I'm going to be your coach."

Kevin gulped. "You are?" he asked nervously.

Suzanne nodded.

Jeremy put his arm around George's shoulders. "Don't worry, buddy. I'll be your coach. Together, we'll win the contest."

"We?" George asked.

"Well, you," Jeremy admitted. "But I'll help you train."

Katie watched as Jeremy and Suzanne stared angrily into each other's eyes. "May the best man win," she said, trying to end the argument.

"Don't worry,

Katie, he will," Jeremy said, pointing to George.

"You mean he will," Suzanne said, pointing to Kevin.

Katie wished her best friends would get along. But she was glad that so many people were interested in Louie's contest.

At lunchtime, Katie sat across from Jeremy and George. George's lunch tray was piled high with two tuna sandwiches, two orders of Tater Tots, two pieces of chocolate cake, and two containers of juice.

"Wow! That's a lot of food," Katie said.

"George is in training," Jeremy told Katie. "He's got to practice eating a lot of food so he can stretch his stomach."

Katie watched as George stuffed half a tuna sandwich into his mouth and chewed.

"Oooh, George," Mandy Banks moaned. "Don't chew with your mouth open. That's gross."

"He can eat any way he wants," Jeremy told her, "as long as he eats a lot."

George shoved six Tater Tots into his mouth. "Yeah," he mumbled with his mouth full.

Just then, Suzanne and Kevin came to the table. As usual, Kevin's tray was stacked high with tomatoes. He also had a tuna sandwich, Tater Tots, and a piece of chocolate cake.

"Okay, Kevin, here's the deal," Suzanne told him. "You have to eat fast so you can get the slices of pizza before anyone else. That means you've got to learn the two-handed munch out."

"The what?" Kevin asked.

"The two-handed munch out," Suzanne repeated. "You have to be able to shove food into your mouth with both hands at the same time."

"Are you nuts?" Kevin asked her in disbelief.

Suzanne put her hands on her hips. "Look, do you want to win this contest or not?"

"I guess so," Kevin said.

"Good," Suzanne said, as she placed a tomato in his left hand, and half a tuna sandwich in his right. "Now go!"

Katie watched as Kevin and George shoved cafeteria food down their throats. They seemed fine at first, but after a while, both boys looked a little sick.

George was the first to stop. "I can't eat another thing," he told Jeremy.

Jeremy stared at George's tray. There were just four Tater Tots left. "I guess you can stop," he said finally. "Besides, we have to go outside. You need to run for a while."

George moaned. "But I just ate."

"Come on," Jeremy said. "You have to be in shape if you're going to be the pizza king."

Suzanne wasn't letting up on Kevin, either. "When you're finished with those tomatoes, we're going outside to work on sit-ups."

"We?" Kevin asked.

"Well, you, actually," Suzanne admitted. "I don't want to get my dress dirty. But I'll count while you crunch."

Kevin just stared at Suzanne.

"Come on, the contest is this Saturday. You need to build strong stomach muscles to eat all that yummy tomato pizza," Suzanne urged, with a smile.

"Don't talk about food right now," Kevin groaned, holding his stomach.

Chapter 8

After several days of stomach stretching, two-hand munching, jogging, sit-ups, and arguments between Suzanne and Jeremy, Saturday finally arrived.

Katie was up and ready to go to the mall before anyone in her family—including her dog, Pepper—was even awake. That rarely happened. Usually, it was the cocker spaniel who woke Katie—with a big wet lick to the face.

Katie wanted to get to the mall as early as possible. She'd promised Louie that she would help him set up for the contest.

"You're awfully quiet this morning,"

Katie's mom said in the car on the way to the mall. "Worried about the contest?"

"I guess," Katie admitted. "What if no one shows up?"

"That won't happen," Mrs. Carew assured her. "There are already a lot of people signed up."

"What if that's not enough? What if Louie still goes out of business?" Katie asked.

"There's nothing you can do about that," her mother said softly. "You've given it your best shot. You're a very good friend to Louie."

Katie wasn't so sure about that. She kept remembering Louie's sad face when he spotted her in Olives and Oregano.

"This just has to work," she insisted.

"Good morning!" Louie greeted Katie with a huge grin as she walked into the pizza shop. He opened the oven door and used the big metal pizza turner to move the pies around. "I've gotten started already. There are four pies in the oven, and a lot more ready to go in later." He pointed to a long line of pre-made, uncooked pizzas. "I've got to make sure the pizzas just keep on coming."

"Mmmm. Smells great," she told Louie. "What do you need me to do?"

"Well, I know the adults are going to want coffee. Can you make sure we have enough sugar and cinnamon out on the counter for anyone who needs it?"

Katie nodded and walked over to the counter. She found a big shaker of a sugar and cinnamon mixture alongside the oregano, hot pepper, and garlic.

"Got it, Louie," she reported back.

"Good," Louie said. "Now, please go into the storeroom and get out lots of paper plates."

Katie did as she was told. As the storeroom door shut behind her, she looked up and down on the shelves, searching for a box of plates.

Suddenly, Katie felt a strange breeze blowing on the back of her neck. It started out gentle enough, but within seconds, the breeze turned into a strong wind.

A wind that was blowing only around Katie.

The magic wind was back!

As the wild tornado swirled faster and faster, Katie grabbed on to a huge, heavy carton of plastic silverware. She held on tight, hoping the heavy box would keep her from blowing away. She squeezed her eyes shut, and hoped that the magic wind would stop blowing soon.

Which is exactly what happened. The wind simply stopped.

Katie opened her eyes slowly and looked around. There were cartons and cans all around her. She was still in the storeroom.

Now she knew where she was. But she still didn't know who she was. Katie looked down at her clothes. Her jeans had been replaced

with baggy white pants. A long white apron covered her stomach.

She looked at her hands. They were large, hairy, and covered with flour. They smelled of garlic.

Katie touched her face. Her fingers brushed over something long and twirly beneath her nose.

Yuck! Katie had a moustache!

Who had Katie become? She picked up a huge, shiny, metal pizza tray and stared at her reflection.

Louie's face stared back at her.

Oh no! The magic wind had turned Katie into Louie!

Katie started to panic. She couldn't possibly be Louie! Not now. All those people out there were going to be expecting Louie's yummy pizzas. Katie didn't know anything about making pizzas. She'd never even cooked anything without her mom before!

The contest was going to be ruined.

Louie was going to have to close the restaurant and move to Florida with his sister. And it would all be Katie's fault.

"Oh, please come back," Katie begged the magic wind. "I need Louie to be here. I want to be me again."

But the magic wind did not return. Which left Katie with no choice. She was going to have to go out there and run Louie's pizza-eating contest.

"This is going to be a disaster," she groaned in her deep, man's voice.

Chapter 9

Katie walked slowly out of the storeroom. Louie's Pizza Shop was still closed. But that hadn't stopped folks from lining up outside the windows. Katie couldn't believe it. There were tons of people there, not to mention television news' crews and newspaper reporters wearing press badges on their shirts.

At any other time, Katie would have been thrilled to see so many people at Louie's. But now she was worried.

Still, Katie couldn't put the contest off any longer. She went over to unlock the door. She could only hope that the pizzas Louie had already made would be enough.

The crowd streamed in. Eight of the ten contestants took their places at the long table that Louie had arranged at the front of the restaurant. The runners—the people Louie had hired to serve the contestants their slices—stood behind the table.

It was almost time for the contest to begin. But there were still two empty seats at the contestants' table.

Suddenly, Becky Stern came leaping and prancing into the pizza shop.

"Here comes George, he's sure to win!" Becky cheered, shaking two black-and-red pom-poms. "Here comes George, he'll make you grin!" She leaped up, did a back flip, and landed in a perfect split.

Jeremy strolled in behind her. "Presenting . . . the one, the only, George 'the Joker' Brennan!" he shouted.

Then George made his entrance. He was dressed in a pair of shiny red shorts and a black T-shirt with a big red smiley face in the middle. He had a black towel tucked into his shirt collar, like a cape. He looked like a superhero.

George smiled at the crowd. He pushed the smiley face on his shirt. A computer chip inside the shirt made a laughing sound.

Some of the photographers leaped in front of George and began snapping his picture. Other people cheered. George was definitely the center of attention.

But not for long. Just then, somebody blew a loud horn. Everyone turned toward the door. There stood Suzanne, holding a plastic horn. She smiled as the attention focused on her.

"Forget that Joker," she told the crowd. "Here's your true champion! Kevin 'Tomato Man' Camilleri!"

Kevin walked in. Unlike George, he seemed embarrassed by all the attention. Maybe that was because of the outfit Suzanne had forced him to wear. He had on red shorts, a red shirt, red knee-socks, and a red hat with a small green felt stem sticking up on the top. He looked like a walking tomato!

Cameras flashed in Kevin's face. His face blushed redder than any tomato.

"Hey, Louie, aren't you going to start the contest?" Ian Camilleri shouted out. "My brother looks awfully hungry."

"So does George," Becky assured Ian. She waved her pom-poms in the air. "Jeremy didn't let him eat a thing for breakfast. Wasn't that smart?" She smiled at Jeremy.

"Can we start the contest, Louie?" Jeremy asked, turning away from Becky.

Katie walked over to the oven, opened the door, and carefully slipped one of the giant pies onto a huge metal spatula, just the way she'd seen Louie do it.

The pizza was heavier than she'd expected. It was big, too. Katie had never held a whole pie before. Whoa! The pizza was sliding off the spatula. Katie shifted her weight and quickly slid it onto one of the big metal pizza trays on the counter.

"That was a close one, Louie," one of the kids in the audience said, laughing.

Katie blushed.

"Boy, that oven must be extra hot today," one of the adults said aloud. "Look how red Louie's face is."

"Come on, Louie, let's get going!" Suzanne pleaded. "Kevin is so ready."

"So's George," Jeremy added.

Working near the big hot pizza oven made Katie very nervous. She wasn't supposed to use any oven without a grown-up. Her mother had made that rule very clear. But she had to break her mother's rule—just this one time.

Katie used a pizza cutter to divide each of the four cooked pies into slices. The ten runners grabbed slices and raced them over to the contestants. As they ate, Katie slid four more of Louie's pre-made pies into the oven.

The contest had begun!

Chapter 10

"Send another one this way, Louie," Jake Lawrence, a teenager who was one of the contestants, called out. Jake had ten empty plates stacked beside him. That meant he'd eaten ten whole slices of pizza. So far, he'd eaten the most.

But Carolyn Evans, a tall thin blond woman, wasn't far behind. She'd eaten nine slices. And Neal Flemming and Bryan Sander had each eaten seven.

"Another slice for my man Kevin, please," Suzanne called out as she patted Tomato Man on the back, and counted the empty plates beside him. Wow! Kevin had eaten six slices.

"Suzanne, I don't think I can eat any more," Kevin groaned.

Suzanne looked at the next table, where George was scarfing down his seventh slice of pizza. "Yes, you can," she said. "You don't want Jeremy . . . I mean, George to beat us, do you?"

"Us?" Kevin asked. "Just how much pizza have you eaten?"

"You know what I mean," Suzanne told him.

"All I know is that if I eat another bite, I'm going to explode." He turned toward where Katie was standing. "Count me out, Louie," he told her.

Katie nodded. She reached over and took away his plates.

The contest had been going on for a while now. Kevin was the fifth contestant to drop out. Jeremy smiled as Kevin waddled away from the table. "Another one down, George," he happily told his client.

George didn't answer. He just kept chewing. But he was slowing down. Finally, he looked up at Jeremy. "I'm sorry," he said, his face turning green. "I think I'm going to be sick!" He jumped up and ran toward the bathroom.

"I'm not feeling too well, either," Bryan Sander added, after taking just one bite of his eighth slice. "I'm done."

"It's down to three!" someone in the crowd shouted out.

Katie looked over toward the counter. There was only one of Louie's pre-made pizzas left, and the three remaining contestants showed no signs of slowing down.

Someone's going to have to make some more pizzas, Katie thought to herself. Then she realized that "someone" was her.

This can't be too hard, Katie tried to convince herself, as she picked up a ball of dough. *I've seen Louie do this a thousand times.*

Katie floured the cooking board, and threw down a ball of dough. She pounded the dough just the way Louie did. Then she stretched out the dough, and tossed it gently in the air. Phew! She caught it.

Katie threw the dough up in the air again. "Wow, this is fun!" she exclaimed as she caught it once again.

Whee! Katie tossed the dough, higher this time, and twirled her body around in circles, just like Louie often did. But Katie wasn't Louie. She had no practice in tossing pizzas. It wasn't so easy to catch the dough as you twirled around.

Plop! The pizza dough landed right on top of Katie's head!

Katie shivered as the thick, damp, raw dough stretched down slowly over her face. It felt all gooey and disgusting—like some sort of weird, edible Halloween mask.

Suddenly, people started applauding. They thought it was a show—like the clowns outside Olives and Oregano.

But Katie knew it wasn't a show. It was a big mistake.

Katie pulled the thick, gooey pizza dough from her head, and threw it in the trash. Then she reached into the refrigerator and pulled out a ball of dough. She floured the counter, and pounded the ball flat. Then she tossed the dough, ever so slightly—she wasn't taking any chances this time.

"Hey, Louie, how 'bout a song?" one of the audience members asked.

Katie gulped. Louie always sang Italian songs while he made pizzas. Katie didn't know any.

"Yeah, come on, Louie!" Ian Camilleri called out.

Katie racked her brain, trying to remember the words to one of Louie's songs. But his songs were always in Italian. The words never meant anything to her.

Finally, Katie sang the only song she knew that might work. She changed the words a little bit, just to make it seem more like something Louie might sing.

"On top of pizza, all covered with cheese," she began. "I lost my poor meatball while somebody sneezed."

The crowd started laughing.

"Boy, Louie's in a funny mood today," Katie heard one teenage boy comment.

"It rolled off the table," Katie continued

singing as she carefully ladled tomato sauce on the circle of dough. "And under a bush. And then my poor meatball was nothing but mush." She sprinkled cheese on the pie.

Katie looked at the finished pizza. It was kind of lopsided, more like an oval than a circle. But there was plenty of sauce and cheese on it. It didn't seem too bad. She opened the oven door.

"Hey, Louie, don't forget your secret spices!" Ian Camilleri shouted out.

A wave of panic washed over Katie. The secret spices! She had no idea what they were. Louie didn't tell anyone what spices he used to make his pizzas different from the rest. That's why they were called *secret*.

But Katie had to do something. Everyone was staring at her. Frantically, she reached out and grabbed the first spice shaker she saw. She sprinkled a brown spice on top of the cheese and sauce, and slid the pizza in the oven.

"That's it for me," a teenager named Jake Lawrence announced as he got up from the table and handed Katie his plate. "I give in."

The crowd applauded for Jake. Katie joined in. He'd eaten ten slices of pizza. That was a pretty good try.

Now there were only two contestants left—Neal Flemming and Carolyn Evans. Katie placed more pizza slices on their plates, and watched nervously as the two competitors chowed down. Those were the last slices Louie had made himself. The next pie was the one Katie had thrown together.

And judging from the strange, unfamiliar smell coming from the oven, that pie was not going to be as good as the real thing.

Chapter 11

Katie opened the oven door and slid the pizza onto a tray. It looked very strange. There was a brown coating on top of the cheese. It looked kind of like melted caramel. Katie hoped the last two contestants wouldn't notice.

But they did. As soon as she placed the fresh slices in front of her, Carolyn sniffed at the air. "Trying something different this time, Louie?" she asked.

Katie just shrugged.

Neal took a bite. "Hey, this is different. It's sweet . . . kind of sugary."

Carolyn bit into her pizza. "I think I taste some cinnamon," she noted.

Katie gulped. Oh no! The brown spice. It must have been the cinnamon and sugar mixture set out for the coffee!

Katie could feel a tear fall from her eye and settle into Louie's moustache. Suddenly, she forgot that she was supposed to be a grown man. She felt very much like the eight-year-old girl she was inside. And so she did a very kid-like thing. She ran into the storeroom, slammed the door, and started to cry.

"Everything's ruined!" she blubbered, as she sat down on one of the cardboard boxes in the storeroom.

Kaboom! The cardboard box collapsed beneath her.

Katie cried harder. Her rear end hurt. Her feet hurt. Her hands were covered with flour, and she was very, very tired.

And for what? When word got out about how bad that last pizza had been, Louie would be out of business. He would have to retire and move away.

Suddenly, without any warning, a fierce wind blasted through the storeroom. The breeze circled around Katie ferociously, like a tornado. Katie shut her eyes tight and grabbed on to a nearby cabinet to keep from being blown away.

The magic wind was back!

There was no way to predict when the wind would come . . . or when it would stop. So Katie wasn't really surprised when the wind died down without any warning.

Slowly, she opened her eyes and looked around. She was still in the storeroom. She felt her face. No moustache. She looked at her hands. They were small, with chipped red nail polish and no flour in the fingernails.

She was Katie Carew again.

And Louie was himself, as well. "What happened?" he moaned. "How did I get in here?"

"Don't you remember?" Katie asked nervously. There was no way she was going to be able to explain about the magic wind to Louie.

"Well, I sort of do," he said. "I mean, I think I remember making a pizza for the contest and . . . " He stopped midsentence and jumped up. "The contest! I've got to get out there!"

Quickly, Katie followed Louie out of the storeroom. Carolyn and Neal were still at the table, chowing down on the pizza Katie had made. Finally, Carolyn leaned back in her chair. "That's it for me," she said slowly. "That cinnamon pizza did me in, Louie."

Louie looked confused.

Katie almost started crying again.

"Hey, then I'm the winner!" Neal cheered. "I'm the pizza king of Cherrydale!"

The photographers' cameras started flashing. A news reporter shoved a microphone into his face. Everyone was cheering.

Everyone but Katie, that is. She was busy staring at Louie. The pizza chef was holding the cinammon and sugar shaker in his hands.

He looked very confused.

Chapter 12

The next morning, Katie tried to stay in bed as late as she could. She didn't want to wake up and face the bad news, so she pretended not to feel Pepper's wet nose on her cheek when he tried to wake her up to play. She covered her ears with her pillow so she couldn't hear her mother's cheerful singing as she cooked breakfast. And she didn't move a muscle when she heard the phone ring in the kitchen.

Katie wasn't getting out of bed. No way. She didn't want to see anyone. She didn't want to talk to anyone.

"Wake up, sleepyhead," Katie's dad said, as

he walked into her room and opened the blinds.

"It's Sunday. I don't have to wake up," Katie moaned.

"You've already had two phone calls," her father told her.

"I don't want to talk to anybody."

"They were from Louie," Katie's dad continued. "He wants you to come down to his store. He said he has something important to say to you."

Katie frowned. Louie wanted to tell her that he was going out of business.

"I'll see you downstairs at breakfast," Katie's dad said. "Mom will drive you to the mall when she goes to work."

Katie wasn't the only kid Louie had called that morning. By the time she and her mother arrived at Louie's Pizza Shop, Suzanne, Jeremy, Becky, George, Kevin, and Ian were already there. They were all sitting at the counter. Suzanne, Jeremy, Becky, and Ian were eating pizza. George and Kevin were eating Italian ices.

"I need a break from pizza," George told Louie.

"Katie, there you are!" Louie gave her a big smile.

He's so brave, Katie thought sadly.

"I have something to tell all of you—especially you, Katie," Louie announced.

Katie gulped. Louie was blaming her for everything. Well, why not? It was her fault, wasn't it?

"Louie, I never meant for . . ." Katie began. But before she could finish her sentence, the phone rang.

Louie reached for the phone. "Louie's Pizza Shop," he said into the receiver. Then he listened to the caller. "No. Not at all. Just come whenever you want," he told the person on the other end.

Louie hung up the phone and grinned. "That's what I wanted to tell you about."

"What?" Katie asked sadly. "Was that the movers coming to get everything?"

"The movers?" Louie asked. "Why would I need movers?"

"Aren't you retiring?" Katie asked him.

"No way," Louie assured her. "That contest was a brilliant idea, Katie. The phone's been ringing all morning. People want deliveries; they want me to cater parties. That call was from a woman asking if she needed a reservation to get a table here!"

"But the cinnamon pizza?" Katie asked. "Wasn't that awful?"

Louie shook his head. "I don't know what made me do that," he said. "But it was great. Did you know that Carolyn Evans is the food reviewer for the *Cherrydale News*? She wrote a whole article about my pizza. It's in today's paper!"

He handed Katie the newspaper. Sure enough, there was a picture of Carolyn eating Louie's pizza.

CHERRYDALE·NEWS

FOOD

PIZZA MAGIC!

LOUIE'S

"Read the last paragraph," Louie said, handing the paper to Katie.

"The best part of the contest was the dessert pizza Louie served," Katie read aloud from the article. "It was sweet and tangy. I'd never had anything like it before. It made losing the contest easier for me to bear. I recommend it to anyone who likes pizza and dessert."

Katie looked up at Louie. "Wow!" she exclaimed.

"I'm adding a dessert pizza to the menu," Louie told the kids. "I think I'll call it the Katie Special."

Wow! A pizza named for her. Katie smiled proudly.

"I've got one in the oven," Louie said. "We can celebrate."

"I'd love a slice!" George exclaimed.

"I thought you were taking a break from pizza," Becky said.

"I did. I didn't eat any all morning," George responded, laughing.

Katie giggled.

As Louie opened the oven door, Katie prepared to feel the heat from the oven. Instead, she felt a cool breeze on the back of her neck.

Oh no! Was the magic wind back? Was it going to turn her into someone else? Right here in front of her friends?

"I'm so glad they finally turned the air-conditioning on in the mall," Suzanne said. "It sure gets hot in here."

Katie sighed with relief. It wasn't the magic wind at all. She was going to be able to sit here and enjoy a Katie Special dessert pizza with her friends. She was Katie Carew and she was going to stay that way.

At least for now.

Pizza Recipe!

You will need:

3 English muffins

1 jar pizza sauce

1 teaspoon oregano

1 12-ounce package of shredded mozzarella

Toppings (sliced pepperoni, sliced
     mushrooms, chopped green pepper,
     meatballs)

2 cookie sheets

Here's what you do: Split each English
muffin in half lengthwise so that you have six
round pizza doughs. Place the muffin halves
on the cookie sheets. Use a spoon to cover
each piece of bread with tomato sauce.

Sprinkle oregano over the sauce. Pile your favorite toppings on each piece. Top each pizza with two tablespoons of shredded mozzarella cheese. Ask an adult to preheat the oven to 325° F. Then have the adult place the cookie sheets in the oven. Bake your pizzas until the cheese is bubbly (about ten minutes). Ask the adult to remove the pizzas from the oven.

Enjoy!

Quiet on the Set!

by Nancy Krulik • illustrated by John & Wendy

Grosset & Dunlap

For Danny, my superstar!—N.K.

For Susan, who is shy,
even to her friends—J&W

Text copyright © 2003 by Nancy Krulik. Illustrations copyright © 2003 by
John and Wendy. All rights reserved. Published by Grosset & Dunlap, a
division of Penguin Young Readers Group, 345 Hudson Street, New York,
New York, 10014. GROSSET & DUNLAP is a trademark of
Penguin Random House LLC.
Manufactured in China

Library of Congress Cataloging-in-Publication Data

Krulik, Nancy E.
  Quiet on the set!! / by Nancy Krulik ; illustrated by John & Wendy.
    p. cm. — (Katie Kazoo, switcheroo ; 10)
Summary: While a movie is being filmed in Cherrydale, Katie switches into
Rosie Moran, a world renowned child actress.
  ISBN 0-448-43214-5 (pbk.)
  [1. Child actors—Fiction. 2. Actors and actresses—Fiction. 3. Magic—
Fiction.] I. John & Wendy, ill. II. Title.
  PZ7.K9416Qu 2003
  [Fic]—dc22

                                              2003017968

                    10 9 8 7 6 5 4 3 2 1

              Proprietary ISBN 978-1-101-95133-0
             Part of Boxed Set, ISBN 978-1-101-95128-6

Chapter 1

"Extra, extra! Read all about it!" Jeremy Fox shouted. "Speedy Escapes!"

"Ooh! You've got the new *3A Times*," Katie Carew said as she took a copy of the newspaper.

"I publish a paper every week," Jeremy told his best friend. "That's the editor's job."

"And you're so good at it," Becky Stern said. "This is the greatest newspaper in the whole school."

Jeremy blushed. He knew Becky liked him—*everyone* knew it. But that didn't mean Jeremy liked her back.

Jeremy turned to Katie. "I think you'll like this article. It's about Speedy."

Katie loved all animals. Her favorite animal was her cocker spaniel, Pepper. But she liked Speedy, the class hamster, too.

George Brennan and Kevin Camilleri raced over to Jeremy. Kevin seemed especially happy to see the new edition of the *3A Times*.

"Did you write about how I was the one who rescued Speedy?" Kevin asked.

"You didn't exactly rescue him," Jeremy said. "He was sitting in the salad bar eating lettuce. You just picked him up and carried him back to the classroom."

Kevin frowned. "Well, if I hadn't gone back to the salad bar for more tomatoes, no one would have found Speedy. We would never have seen him again."

Becky got a funny look on her face. "I'm never going to eat at the salad bar again. Who knows what that hamster did in there!"

"Ooh, that *is* gross," Jeremy agreed.

Sharing the salad bar with Speedy didn't seem to bother Kevin. "No one—not even Speedy—is going to keep me from my tomatoes!" he declared.

"Kevin's right," George said. "Nothing Speedy did could be worse than the big bug I found in my cake last week."

"You found a bug in your cake?" Katie asked.

George nodded. "I guess it was the fly's day off!" He started laughing.

Katie giggled. She loved George's jokes.

"Hi, you guys!" Suzanne Lock shouted as she dashed across the playground to join the other kids in class 3A.

Suzanne was wearing a long green skirt, suede boots, and a shimmery pink shirt. Her hair was piled high on her head. She looked like she was going to a fancy party.

"Wow, you look so cool!" Katie said, complimenting her.

Suzanne grinned. "Thanks."

"Why are you dressed so fancy?" Becky asked.

"It's my current events day," Suzanne told her.

"Is that all?" George said. "You don't have

to get all dressed up to do your current events. I never do."

"Me, neither," Kevin agreed. "I don't dress up for anything."

"Well, *I* try to look good all the time," Suzanne told them. "You never know when a movie producer could be looking for a new star."

Jeremy rolled his eyes. Sometimes Suzanne really annoyed him. This was one of those times. Jeremy and Suzanne were both Katie's best friends, but that didn't mean they liked each other very much.

"What are you talking about, Suzanne?" Jeremy asked her.

"You'll find out," Suzanne assured him. "It's part of my current events report. And I guarantee my news will beat anything in the *3A Times*!"

Chapter 2

Katie sat in the classroom and stared at the clock. It was only 11:33. She tried to focus on the problems in her math textbook. But her eyes kept going back to the numbers on the clock. Katie couldn't wait for 11:45. That was current events time. She was dying to find out what Suzanne's news story was.

The other kids were having trouble waiting for current events time, too. Everyone seemed to be watching the clock . . . and Suzanne.

Katie knew Suzanne was happy everyone was watching her. There were two things Suzanne really loved—being the center of

attention, and knowing something no one else knew. Today, Suzanne had both of those things.

Finally, Mrs. Derkman put away her math textbook, and took a seat behind her big desk in the front of the room.

"Okay, class, whose turn is it for current events?"

"Suzanne's!" everyone shouted out at once.

Suzanne stood up and walked slowly toward the front of the room.

"Come on, Suzanne, tell us what the big deal is," George said as she walked past his desk.

"Yeah, what's this great news you have for us?" Kevin added.

But Suzanne didn't hurry. She liked making everyone wait for her surprise.

"Okay," she said, taking a dramatic breath. "Here's the big story. Some famous Hollywood producers are making a movie in Cherrydale."

"Why would anyone make a movie here?"

George asked. "There's nothing special about Cherrydale."

"That's the point," Suzanne said. "They wanted an average American town. And you guys haven't heard the best part. This movie stars Rosie Moran!"

Rosie Moran was the most famous kid in the whole world. She was a big movie star, even though she was only nine years old. The kids had all seen her movies.

So had Mrs. Derkman. "I love Rosie Moran!" the teacher blurted out.

"You go to Rosie Moran movies?" George asked her, surprised.

Mrs. Derkman nodded. "I've seen *all* her movies. *Camp Capers, Camp Capers 2,* and *Sleepover Summer.* But my favorite Rosie Moran movie is her first one— *Scary School Day.*"

Suzanne continued her report. "The name of the movie is *The Kids Are in Charge*. In this movie, the parents in a small town switch places with their kids. The adults go to school, and the kids go to work."

"Oh, that sounds marvelous!" Mrs. Derkman gushed. "I can just see Rosie Moran playing the head of a big company. Or a firefighter. Ooh! Maybe they'll let her play a teacher!"

Katie didn't think the movie sounded marvelous. She thought it sounded awful. Katie didn't like anything that had to do with switching places.

That was because Katie had done a lot of switching recently.

It had all started one day a few weeks ago. Katie had spilled mud on her favorite jeans, lost the football game for her team, and let out a massive burp in front of the entire class.

On that day, Katie had wished she could be anyone but herself.

There must have been a shooting star flying overhead when she made that wish, because the very next day, the magic wind came. The magic wind was a wild tornado that blew only around Katie. It was so strong that it had the power to turn Katie into someone else.

The first time the magic wind came, it turned Katie into Speedy, the class hamster. She'd spent the whole morning gnawing on chew sticks, running on the hamster wheel, and trying to escape from Speedy's cage. She was so glad when the magic wind returned and turned her back into Katie Carew.

But Katie hadn't stayed herself for very long. The magic wind came back again and again. It had already turned her into other kids, like Suzanne's baby sister Heather, Becky Stern, and Jeremy Fox. One time, the magic wind turned her into Mr. Kane, the school principal. Another time, it turned her into Lucille, the lunch lady in the cafeteria.

Katie never knew when the magic wind would come back again. All Katie knew was that when it did, she was going to wind up getting into some sort of trouble—and so would the person she'd turn into.

That's why Katie didn't think a movie about kids who switch places with adults would be very good. There was nothing funny about switcheroos.

Chapter 3

Katie might not have thought that *The Kids Are in Charge* sounded like a good movie, but the other kids sure were excited. It was all they could talk about at lunch.

"Today, they're filming a scene on Main Street, in front of the pet shop," Suzanne told the kids at their lunch table. "My mother said I could go there after school. I hope I can meet the director."

"I hope I can meet Rosie Moran," Mrs. Derkman interrupted.

The kids all looked up in shock. Mrs. Derkman never sat with them at lunch. But

there she was, putting her lunch tray down beside Kevin.

Kevin moved his chair as far as he could away from the teacher.

"I've heard Rosie's just like a normal kid," Mandy Banks said.

"My magazine says she likes skating and guitar," Miriam added.

"I read that her favorite color is blue," Mrs. Derkman chimed in.

The kids all stared at her.

"Katie, do you want to come to Main Street with me?" Suzanne asked.

Katie didn't want to be anywhere near *The Kids Are in Charge*—in case it gave the magic wind any ideas. But she couldn't explain that to Suzanne. So she said, "I guess I can go for a little while."

After school, Katie and her friends headed over to Main Street.

"Wow! Would you look at this!" Jeremy exclaimed.

"I've never seen Main Street this busy!" Katie added.

Usually, Main Street was a quiet place, with people walking down the sidewalk and a few cars parked on the street. But today people with walkie-talkies ran on the side-walk. Big trucks with lights were parked near the pet shop. And everywhere you looked there were huge trailers.

"Those are the stars' dressing rooms," Suzanne told her friends.

"I wonder which trailer belongs to Rosie Moran?" Miriam asked as the kids tried to peek inside the windows.

Suddenly a man in a black leather jacket jumped in front of Katie and her friends. "You kids have to wait here. They're about to film the next scene."

"Right now?" Suzanne asked excitedly.

The man in the jacket nodded. "Any second now Rosie is going to walk out of that pet shop and onto the street. If you're real quiet you can watch."

The kids all stared at the door of the pet shop. A woman stood in front of the shop with a big black clapboard. "Scene twelve, take three," she said. Then she opened the top of the board and clapped it down.

Rosie Moran walked out of the pet shop. She looked like she was about to cry. "I wish Mr. Marks was here. He'd know what to do,"

she said. A tear fell down her cheek.

"And . . . cut!" the director shouted. "That was perfect, Rosie."

"Thank goodness," Rosie moaned. "I don't want to have to cry again today." She turned and ran toward her trailer. But before she could reach the door, Miriam jumped in front of her.

"Rosie, I'm your biggest fan," Miriam gushed. "Can I have your autograph?"

Rosie shook her head. Her long chocolate brown curls bounced all around her. "Get out of my way."

Miriam looked as though she'd been slapped across the face. "But I just want your autograph. I love all your movies."

"Everyone says that," Rosie snapped back. "Can't you come up with anything more original?"

"The magazines all said you were nice," Miriam sobbed.

"Don't believe everything you read," Rosie shouted. She stormed into her trailer and slammed the door.

Chapter 4

As the kids stood on the sidewalk, they could hear Rosie shouting from inside her trailer. "I told them not to let anyone on the set!" she screamed. "How am I supposed to think with all those kids around?"

Miriam sobbed harder.

"Don't cry," Katie urged her classmate. "She's not worth it."

"I'm never going to see any of her movies again," Mandy promised.

"None of us will," Jeremy said.

Suzanne looked at her classmates. "I'll see this movie," she told them.

The kids all stared at Suzanne with surprise.

"I'll see it if I get to be in it," Suzanne explained.

George laughed. "Guess you won't be seeing it, either, then."

Suzanne stuck her tongue out at him.

Just then a woman with dark, short hair and glasses burst out of Rosie's dressing room. "I'm really sorry about that," she apologized. "Rosie is usually so nice to her fans. She's a little cranky today."

Katie frowned. A little cranky? Rosie had been *mean*!

"I just spoke to her," the woman continued. "She's sorry."

"Are you Rosie's mother?" Katie asked.

"Oh, no. I'm Amy Edmunds, Rosie's assistant," the woman explained kindly. "Rosie would really like to make it up to you. In fact, she's on the phone right now, asking the director to let all of you be extras in the movie."

Jeremy looked at her curiously. "Extra whats?" he asked.

Suzanne rolled her eyes. "You'll have to forgive him," she said. "He doesn't know anything about the *biz*."

"Oh, and you do?" Jeremy asked.

"I know that extras are actors who stand in the background to make the scene look real," Suzanne told him.

"Exactly," Amy agreed. "Rosie would like you all to be extras in the scene we're filming Saturday." She pulled some papers from her clipboard. "Have your parents sign these permission slips. Be at the park on Saturday morning."

Just then, Mrs. Derkman came running over. "Did you kids meet Rosie Moran?" the teacher asked excitedly.

"We met her, all right." George frowned.

"Was she just like we expected?" Mrs. Derkman continued.

"Not exactly," Katie began.

"She's *better* than we expected," Suzanne interrupted excitedly. "She invited us all to be extras in *The Kids Are in Charge*!"

"How wonderful!" Mrs. Derkman exclaimed. She turned to Amy Edmunds. "Is there room for one more?" she asked.

Amy shook her head. "Sorry, kids only."

Mrs. Derkman looked like she was about to cry!

Chapter 5

That evening, Katie and her mother went to the Cherrydale Mall to the Book Nook bookstore, where Katie's mom works. There was a big shipment of books coming in, and Mrs. Carew had to make sure they were all put out on the right shelves.

"Why don't you go to Louie's Pizza Shop?" Katie's mom said. "You can do your homework there."

Katie smiled. Math homework wouldn't be so awful if she could do it while she bit into Louie's secret sauce and extra gooey cheese. "See you later," she called to her mom.

"Hi, Katie," Louie said as Katie walked

into the pizza shop. "Is your mom working tonight?"

Katie nodded. "She said I should wait for her here."

"It's crowded, but I think you can find a table in the back," Louie told Katie. "I'll bring you a slice in a minute."

"Thanks, Louie," Katie said.

Katie sat down and took out her math book. She tried hard to concentrate, but the people at the table behind her were having a loud argument.

"This just isn't a good time," one woman said.

"But it's what she wants," the other woman argued.

"I'm her mother. I know what's best for her!" the first woman shouted.

"Why are you two talking about me like I'm not around?" the girl at the table said.

Katie's eyes flew open wide. She'd know that voice anywhere. The girl sitting behind her was Rosie Moran!

"Mom, I don't want to quit acting. I love acting. But I need a break," Rosie pleaded. "I want to be a normal kid for once. At least for a little while."

"You're *not* a normal kid," Rosie's mother argued. "You're a star. Besides, you have to finish this movie. I've already signed the contract."

Rosie leaped up from the table and ran sobbing into the bathroom.

Katie had been mad at Rosie for the way she'd treated Miriam. But now she felt really sorry for her. Quickly, she followed Rosie into the bathroom.

The bathroom looked empty. But Katie could hear sniffling coming from one of the stalls.

"Are you okay?" Katie called out.

"Go away," Rosie snapped back.

"I just thought you could use a friend," Katie answered.

"I don't have any friends."

"Sure you do," Katie said. "I'll be your friend."

Slowly, Rosie opened the door to the stall. "Weren't you one of the kids on the set today?" she asked Katie.

Katie nodded.

"So why do you want to be friends with me? I wasn't very nice."

"That's true," Katie agreed. "But everybody gets in a bad mood sometimes."

"I'm in a bad mood a lot," Rosie admitted.

"Maybe you're working too hard. I get that way when I have too much homework," Katie said.

"I don't have any homework," Rosie told her.

"Don't you go to school?" Katie asked.

"Sort of," Rosie explained. "I have a tutor. She teaches me when I'm on the set."

"Just you?" Katie asked. "No other kids?"

Rosie nodded. "It's just me and her. But I wish I went to school like you. I'll bet it's fun."

Katie thought about that. Mrs. Derkman's classroom wasn't always a fun place to be. But at least there was lunchtime and recess.

Just then, Katie got a great idea. "How long are you going to be in Cherrydale?" she asked Rosie.

"Until Sunday," Rosie answered.

"Well, how about coming to my school for the rest of the week?" Katie asked her.

Rosie shook her head. "I can't just go to a school for one week," she said. "Your teacher wouldn't let me."

Katie thought about how Mrs. Derkman had spent the whole day talking about Rosie Moran. "I'll bet she would," she assured Rosie.

"It would be a lot of fun," Rosie admitted.

"Then it's a deal," Katie said. "Meet me at Cherrydale Elementary School tomorrow morning."

"Okay," Rosie agreed.

Katie started to leave.

"Hey," Rosie called after her. "I don't even know your name."

"It's Katie Carew," Katie told her. "But you can call me Katie Kazoo. All my friends do."

"Okay, *Katie,*" Rosie told her. "I'll see you tomorrow."

Chapter 6

"Do you really think she'll come?"
Suzanne asked Katie as the two girls sat in
the school playground early the next morning.

"I hope so," Katie told her.

Just then, a big black limousine pulled up
in the school parking lot.

"She's here!" Katie shouted.

A tall man in a blue uniform leaped out of
the driver's seat of the limo. He opened the
back door and stood to the side. Rosie got out
of the car.

"Thanks, Frank," she said to the driver.
"School's over at three o'clock. You can come
get me then."

"Very good, Miss Moran," Frank said.

As Frank drove away, Rosie walked toward the bench where Katie and Suzanne were sitting.

"Hi, Katie Kazoo," she greeted Katie.

"Hi, Rosie," Katie replied. "I'm so glad you could come. I thought maybe your mother wouldn't let you."

"She almost didn't. But I convinced her that we could tell some of the fan magazines about my time in regular school. She liked that."

"Ahem!" Suzanne interrupted. "Aren't you forgetting something, Katie?"

Katie blushed. "Oh, I'm sorry. Rosie, this is Suzanne Lock."

"Nice to meet you, Suzanne," Rosie said.

"I think we'll be good friends," Suzanne told her. "We have a lot in common."

"We do?" Rosie asked.

"Sure," Suzanne assured her. "We're both actresses."

"Cool!" Rosie said. "What kind of acting do you do? Movies or the stage?"

Suzanne blushed. "Well, nothing yet. But I'm on the verge of getting an acting job."

"Oh, right," Katie remembered. "We're all going to be extras in your new movie," she said to Rosie.

"Well, that's just a start," Suzanne said. "I meant bigger parts, of course."

"I'm sure you're a great actress," Rosie assured Suzanne. Then she turned to Katie. "Are you sure your teacher won't mind having me in class for a few days?"

"Oh, no," Katie assured her. "I asked her all about it last night."

Rosie seemed confused. "You saw your teacher last night?" she asked.

Katie nodded. "She's my next door neighbor."

"Your teacher is your neighbor!" Rosie exclaimed. "That's really cool."

Suzanne laughed. "Cool is not a word I would use to describe Mrs. Derkman."

"Oh," Rosie said. "What is she like?"

"See for yourself." Katie pointed across the playground. Mrs. Derkman was running across the pavement.

Katie and Suzanne stared at their teacher. They'd never even seen her walk fast before,

never mind run.

"Yoo-hoo! Rosie!" Mrs. Derkman shouted. "Hello."

Rosie jumped to her feet. "Hello," she said quietly.

"Oh, I can hardly believe you're here," Mrs. Derkman exclaimed. "You're even more beautiful in real life. And I love the outfit you're wearing."

Suzanne and Katie studied Rosie's clothes. She was wearing black stretch jeans, a leopard pattern shirt, and a leather jacket with fringe. She did look pretty cool.

"I think that's probably the most fashionable thing anyone has ever worn at Cherrydale Elementary School," Mrs. Derkman gushed.

Suzanne let out a tiny gasp.

"You look fantastic, too, Suzanne," Katie interrupted, trying to soothe her friend. "I love that headband. And your shoes are really cool."

But nothing could make Suzanne feel

better. She glared angrily at Rosie.

"Well, I see the other children are coming," Mrs. Derkman told Rosie. "Why don't we line up and get an early start? It would be terrific to get a couple of extra minutes of learning in this morning."

"Okay." Rosie smiled at Mrs. Derkman.

"Just what we need, extra learning time," Suzanne hissed as Rosie and Mrs. Derkman walked off together.

"It's not her fault," Katie said.

"No, it's not," Suzanne agreed. "It's yours."

"Mine?" Katie asked.

"You invited her here," Suzanne reminded her.

"Come on, it's no big deal," Katie said. "Besides, you wanted Rosie to come today, too."

"I don't know, Katie," Suzanne said as she stared at Rosie's leather jacket and stretch jeans. "I think this was a bad idea."

Chapter 7

"Rosie, why don't you sit in the empty desk in the first row?" Mrs. Derkman suggested.

Rosie sat down next to Jeremy and smiled. Jeremy blushed.

"Okay, class, let's go back to talking about verbs. Everybody pull out your grammar books," Mrs. Derkman said.

Rosie raised her hand shyly. "I don't have any books," she said.

"You can share with Jeremy," the teacher answered.

It was easy to see that Jeremy was excited to share his book with a movie star!

Becky's face burned red. She didn't like

that Rosie was sharing with Jeremy. She *especially* didn't like how glad Jeremy was to do it.

"Who can tell me what a verb is?" Mrs. Derkman asked.

Kevin raised his hand. "It's an action word . . ." he began.

Before Kevin could finish his sentence, Rosie began to sing. "Herb the Verb is a man of action. He's busy all day through. He hops and walks, giggles and talks. He does whatever we do."

Everyone in the class stared at Rosie. They waited for Mrs. Derkman to yell at her.

But Mrs. Derkman didn't yell. Instead, she said, "What a lovely song."

"There's a dance that goes with it," Rosie told her.

The class watched with amazement as Rosie began to hop around the room. When she reached the front of the room again, she did a flip in the air, and landed on one leg.

Mrs. Derkman applauded. "Isn't it exciting to have such a talented gymnast visit us?" Mrs. Derkman asked the class.

Now Becky was *really* angry. She'd been studying gymnastics since she was a little girl. She was a lot better than Rosie.

"That looks like fun!" George jumped up and twirled in a circle. He bent his knee and stuck his leg out behind him. "Look at me! I'm Herb the Verb!"

The class laughed. George looked like the world's goofiest ballerina.

"George!" Mrs. Derkman exclaimed. "Take your seat immediately."

"How come she gets to dance?" he asked the teacher.

"Rosie was teaching us a way to remember what a verb is," the teacher replied. "You're just being silly. Now sit down, or you will lose recess today."

George plopped down in his chair. He had a very grumpy look on his face.

"How much longer is she staying here?" he hissed angrily at Katie.

Chapter 8

At lunchtime, Katie walked with Rosie to the cafeteria.

"You eat here every day?" Rosie asked Katie with a frown.

"Sure."

"It's not what I expected," Rosie said, looking around. "I thought it would be more like the restaurant at the movie studio."

"What's that like?" Katie asked.

"Well, there are a lot of tables, and you get your food on line, like here," Rosie said. "But it's decorated with flowers and plants. There are cloth napkins and real silverware, not plastic. And the food smells a lot better."

"Well, you wanted to go to a real school," Katie reminded her. "This is real school food."

Rosie smiled. "You're right. It *is* fun here," she told Katie. "And your teacher is *so* nice."

Katie raised her eyebrow, but she didn't say anything. Nice was not a word most kids would use to describe Mrs. Derkman. Then again, Mrs. Derkman was treating Rosie a lot differently than she treated the rest of her students.

After the girls had loaded their trays with macaroni and cheese, chocolate pudding, and milk, they walked over toward a table in the corner. Some of the kids from class 3A were already sitting there.

"Katie, I saved you a seat!" Suzanne called out.

"Squeeze over," Katie asked Suzanne. "Rosie needs to sit, too."

"Sorry, no room," Suzanne said. "She can sit over there." Suzanne pointed toward the

other side of the table where Jeremy was
sitting.

"It's okay, Katie," Rosie said. "I don't
mind."

But before Rosie could sit down, Becky
moved to the seat next to Jeremy.

Rosie shrugged and sat down where Becky
had been sitting. That put her right
across from George.

"Rosie, maybe you don't
want to . . ." Katie
began. She wanted to

warn her not to sit near George. He could be really gross at lunch.

"Leave her alone," Suzanne interrupted. "Serves her right."

Everyone started eating. Everyone but George, that is. He was busy rolling pieces of bread into little balls. He launched one of the bread balls toward the end of the table. It landed right on top of Miriam's macaroni.

"Ooh! Gross. You rolled that ball in your dirty fingers," Miriam moaned. "Now how am I supposed to eat my lunch?"

George threw a bread ball at Kevin. Kevin didn't think the ball was gross. He picked it

up off the table and popped it in his mouth.

Suzanne and Miriam looked like they were going to throw up. But Rosie wasn't grossed out at all. "He's funny," Rosie said.

"George is the funniest guy in our whole class," Kevin told her. "Maybe even in our whole school."

George smiled proudly.

"You like jokes?" Rosie asked him.

George nodded.

"Have you heard this one?" Rosie asked. "What kind of star wears fancy sunglasses and drives an expensive car?"

"I don't know," George said.

"A movie star!" Rosie joked. She started to laugh.

So did Kevin. "That's pretty funny," he said. "It looks like George has some competition."

George frowned and threw another ball of bread at Kevin.

Kevin picked up the bread ball and got ready to throw it back at George. But before

he could, Mrs. Derkman arrived at the table. "Are you kids playing soccer after lunch?" the teacher asked.

Jeremy nodded. "We're playing against the kids in class 3B."

"Who are the captains?" Mrs. Derkman asked.

"Jeremy and Andrew Epstein," Kevin told her.

Mrs. Derkman thought about that for a moment. "Why don't we let our guest be the captain of our team today?"

"Jeremy is our best player," Becky said, butting in.

"Yes," Mrs. Derkman agreed. "But I'll bet Rosie has never been a soccer captain."

"I've never even *played* soccer," Rosie admitted.

"Well, today you'll play," Mrs. Derkman assured her. "I'm sure you'll make a great captain."

As the teacher walked away, Jeremy turned

to Kevin. "Oh, great," he complained. "A captain who doesn't even know how to play. We're going to lose for sure." Jeremy glared at Rosie. He hated losing.

"Katie, why did you have to invite her to our school?" Suzanne whispered. "She's ruining everything!"

"Shhh," Katie warned. "She'll hear you."

But Rosie had already heard Suzanne. She jumped up from the table and ran toward the bathroom. Katie followed right behind her.

"Funny how we keep meeting in bathrooms," Katie joked as the two girls stood alone by the sinks.

Rosie didn't smile. "This is all your fault!" she yelled at Katie.

"What is?"

"The kids all hate me," Rosie told her.

"No, they don't," Katie said. " It's just hard being the new kid. George went through the same thing when he moved here. Becky did, too."

Rosie sobbed. "My mother was right. I can't be a normal kid."

"Sure you can," Katie assured her. "You just have to stay at a school for more than a few days. Then you'll become just one of the kids."

"I'm never going to have friends."

"But I'm your friend," Katie reminded her.

"No, you're not," Rosie said. "This is the

worst day of my whole life, and you did it to me!" She stormed out of the bathroom.

× × ×

After school, Rosie got into her big limo and drove away. She never even waved good-bye.

"I hope we never see her again," George said.

"Yeah," Jeremy agreed. "We got killed in soccer today."

"I'll see her again," Suzanne said.

"You will?" Katie asked. "I thought you hated her."

"I do," Suzanne agreed. "But I'm still going to be in her movie."

"Suzanne . . ." Katie started.

"Oh, come on, Katie. We have to go to the set on Saturday."

"*We?*" Katie asked.

"Sure." Suzanne threw her arm around Katie. "I want my best friend there when I become a star!"

Chapter 9

On Saturday morning, Katie and Suzanne walked over to the park together. Katie was wearing a pair of purple jeans with laces on the side, and a white shirt. Suzanne was wearing a shimmery blue dress, long, dangly earrings, and a feather boa.

"I thought we were supposed to wear our regular clothes," Katie said.

"These are my regular clothes," Suzanne argued.

"That boa is from last Halloween," Katie reminded her. "And you wore that dress to your cousin's wedding."

"So what? I'm a star. I want the director to

notice me right away."

Katie looked at Suzanne's big earrings and her feather boa. "Oh, he'll notice you," she assured her.

Suzanne lifted her head high. "Oh, and one thing," she told Katie. "If the director asks, my name isn't Suzanne Lock."

"It isn't?"

Suzanne shook her head. "From now on I'm Suzanne Superstar!"

"You changed your name?"

Suzanne nodded. "It's my stage name. All us movie stars have them."

The other kids were already on the set by the time Suzanne and Katie got to the park. Like Suzanne, they didn't care how much they disliked Rosie. They just wanted to be in a movie!

Becky, Miriam, and Mandy were looking at the giant cameras and lights. Jeremy was kicking a can around the park. George and

Kevin were at the food table. Rosie was sitting on the steps of her trailer. She did not want to talk to any of the kids from class 3A.

"Okay, everyone, let's get started," a tall man in a baseball cap called out. "I'm Carl Swenson, the director of this movie."

Carl looked out at the kids in front of him. His eyes stopped at Suzanne. "What are you wearing?" he asked her.

"This old thing?" Suzanne asked sweetly. "It's just something I pulled from my closet. Do you like it?"

Carl shook his head. "It's all wrong. Run over to the green trailer and see if there's something the costume people have for you."

Katie thought that would make Suzanne mad. But Suzanne seemed really happy.

"I'm getting a costume!" she whispered excitedly to Katie.

After a few minutes, Suzanne came out of the trailer. She did not look happy anymore. Suzanne was dressed in a pair of old overalls.

She looked very regular.

"Now we can begin," Carl said. "You kids walk around and pretend to enjoy the day. Then Rosie will come out and say her lines. Everybody understand?"

The children nodded.

"Good," Carl said. "Let's shoot the scene."

A woman with a clapboard stood in front of the camera. "Park scene, take one," she said.

Katie and her friends walked quietly around the park, looking at the trees and smiling at each other. Then Rosie walked in front of the camera. She looked beautiful in her short green dress. Her makeup made her eyes look even bigger and bluer than usual.

Rosie opened her mouth to speak. Suzanne did a flying leap across the grass, and landed right beside her.

"Cut!" Carl shouted. He turned to Suzanne. "What did you do?"

"My character is a dancer," Suzanne explained sweetly. "She's flying through the air to celebrate this day."

Carl's face turned red. "Your character is a normal, everyday kid. There's no dancing . . . uh . . . what's your name?" he asked.

"Suzanne Superstar," Suzanne answered.

"More like Super*weird*," George joked.

Everyone laughed. Even Rosie.

"Let's try this again," Carl said. "Action!"

Once again the kids walked around the park. Rosie stepped in front of the camera.

"Hi, there!" Suzanne yelled out. "Isn't this a gorgeous day?"

"Cut!" Carl shouted. "What are you doing? You're an extra. Extras don't speak."

"It isn't normal for kids to be quiet in the park," Suzanne corrected him. "I was trying to help make it more real."

Carl's face was really red now. "You know how you can help?" he shouted.

"How?" Suzanne asked eagerly.

"You can leave."

Suzanne stared at him. "What?" she asked.

"You can leave," he repeated. "Every minute we waste costs the studio thousands of dollars. I can't afford to keep stopping for you. You're fired."

Suzanne's eyes opened wide. She turned

beet red, and started to cry. Then she raced off the set.

Katie ran after her. "Wait up," she said as she ran into a wooded part of the park. But Suzanne was too fast. Before Katie could reach her, Suzanne was out of the park and on her way home.

Katie stood there, all alone in the woods. Suddenly, she felt a cool wind blowing on the back of her neck. Katie looked up at the trees. The leaves were still. She looked down at the grass. Not a blade was moving.

Oh, no! The magic wind was back.

Within seconds, the wind was swirling around her like a giant tornado. Katie felt like she could be blown away. Quickly, she grabbed on to a tree and shut her eyes tightly.

And then it stopped. Just like that.

Slowly, Katie opened her eyes and looked around. She was still in the park.

Okay, so now she knew where she was. But she didn't know *who* she was.

Just then a woman with a clipboard and a walkie-talkie came up beside her. "I've found her," she said into her walkie-talkie. Then she turned to Katie. "You'd better hurry back, Rosie," she said. "Carl's getting really mad!"

Chapter 10

Before Katie knew what was going on, the woman with the clipboard was dragging her back onto the movie set.

"But I can't . . ." Katie began. Then she stopped herself. She couldn't tell this woman that she wasn't really Rosie Moran. She would never believe her. Katie wouldn't believe it either if it weren't happening to her.

"Rosie's back," Carl said as Katie stood in front of the camera. "Let's get to work, people. Time is money! Makeup, get rid of that shine on her nose!"

A man jumped in front of Katie. He pushed a big powder puff in her face. Chalky

white powder flew in her mouth and up her nose. Katie coughed hard.

Before Katie could catch her breath, a woman snapped a clapboard right in front of her. "Park scene, take three!"

"Action!" Carl shouted.

Katie gulped. She didn't know what to do. She didn't know how to be a movie star. The only thing she'd ever seen stars do was walk down the red carpet before awards shows.

So, that's what Katie did. She raised her head high, smiled at the camera, and waved at imaginary fans. Then she spun around in a circle, showing her make-believe gown to the invisible photographers.

"Cut!" Carl yelled. "What are you doing?"

Katie shrugged. "I'm acting like a movie star."

"Why?"

"Because I *am* a movie star. I'm Rosie Moran."

Carl sighed. "In real life, you are. But in

this movie, you're just a kid. Now say your line and we can move on."

Katie gulped. She had no idea what Rosie's line was. "I don't know what to say," she admitted.

"No, no, no!" Carl yelled. "The line is, 'I do wish I could go back in time and reverse things'."

Katie wrinkled her nose. "That's what I'm supposed to say?"

Carl nodded.

"But no kid talks like that."

"You do in this film," Carl barked at her. "And . . . action!"

Katie smiled brightly into the camera. "I do wish I could go back in time and reverse things," she said.

Carl's face turned bright red. "No! No! No!" he shouted.

"I said the line," Katie told him.

"True," Carl admitted angrily. "But why are you smiling?"

Katie had never heard a grown-up yell so loudly. Her eyes welled up with tears.

"That's better," Carl said. "I want to see crying. Lots of crying."

A tear dripped down Katie's cheek.

"Perfect," Carl said. "Keep going. Action!"

Katie cried so hard that her nose began to run. She wiped it with her sleeve.

"Cut!" Carl screamed.

"That's disgusting. Somebody get Rosie a tissue!"

Katie sobbed harder.

Carl turned to the cameraman. "My agent warned me not to work with kids," he said.

"Can I try it again?" Katie whispered.

"Do we have a choice?" Carl barked back.

The makeup man shoved the powder puff in Katie's face again.

The woman with the clapboard shouted, "Park scene, take six."

"Action!" Carl ordered.

Katie opened her mouth to speak. But before she could say a word, George started to scream. "Yuck! A pigeon just pooped on my head."

Everyone started to laugh, even Katie. In fact, she giggled so hard she couldn't stop. Tears of laughter poured out of her eyes.

George started running around the park, waving his hands wildly. "Get it off! Get it off!" he screamed.

Katie laughed so hard she fell down on the ground. She rolled around on the grass, clutching her side.

"Rosie! Stand up!" Carl shouted. "You're ruining your costume!"

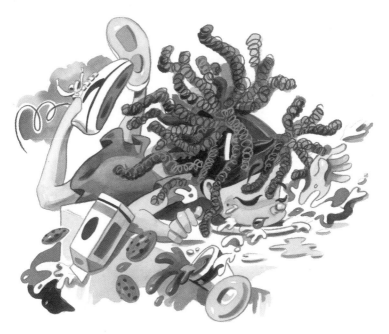

Katie couldn't stop giggling. She tried to stand up, and she tripped over her own feet.

Bam! She fell right into the food table. Her face landed in a lemon meringue pie. Big blobs of yellow and white goo dripped down her cheeks and onto Rosie's costume.

"That's it!" Carl declared. "Wait until the people in California hear about this. You'll never work again, Rosie Moran!"

Chapter 11

That was enough to stop Katie's giggles. She'd ruined Rosie Moran's career!

Katie ran into a nearby trailer and locked the door. Rosie's mother banged on the door. But Katie wouldn't let her in. She didn't want another adult yelling at her.

As she sat alone in Rosie's trailer, Katie understood why Rosie had said she'd needed to take a break and be a normal kid. Acting wasn't all red carpets and famous people. It was memorizing lines, and spending long days on movie sets. There was no time for play-ing—or even laughing.

Just then, Katie felt a cool breeze on the

back of her neck. She looked around. There were no windows in the trailer. And the door was locked tight.

There was only one reason that breeze was blowing.

The magic wind was back!

"Why couldn't you have come ten minutes ago!" Katie shouted angrily.

As if to answer her, the magic wind blew

harder, circling around her like a furious tornado. Katie shut her eyes tight as the wind blew stronger and stronger.

And then, suddenly, it stopped. Slowly, Katie opened her eyes. She wasn't in the trailer anymore. She was back in the park. She looked down. She was wearing her purple jeans again.

"There you are, Katie Kazoo!" George shouted as he, Kevin, Jeremy, and Becky walked toward her.

"Where have you been?" Jeremy asked her. "You missed it."

"Rosie Moran messed up big time!" Kevin laughed. "You should have seen her with that pie in her hair. She looked like she didn't know what had happened."

Katie sighed. Rosie probably had no idea what had happened to her. But Katie did. After all, she was the one who'd really tripped into the food table.

"Serves her right," Becky added.

"Come on, guys, Rosie probably feels awful," Katie argued.

"How do you know?" Becky asked her.

"I know it's not easy being Rosie. I know she works hard. And I know that director is a mean guy," Katie told her.

"How do you know all that?" Jeremy asked.

"Because I . . ." Katie stopped herself. She couldn't tell him how she knew what it was like being Rosie. So instead she said, "I'm sure it wasn't all Rosie's fault."

"That's true," Kevin agreed. "George made her laugh."

"I had pigeon poop in my hair," George insisted.

"It doesn't matter who started it," Jeremy said. "Rosie's career is over."

"Not necessarily . . ." Katie began.

"Uh-oh," Jeremy interrupted. "It sounds like Katie's got another one of her ideas."

Chapter 12

"So tell me again why we want to help Rosie Moran?" Jeremy asked Katie. It was Sunday morning. Rosie was supposed to fly back to California soon. Katie, Jeremy, Suzanne, Becky, Mandy, Miriam, and George were all sitting in the lobby of the Cherrydale Plaza hotel, waiting to catch her before she left.

"Because we were mean to her," Katie said. "We made her feel awful at school."

"But Mrs. Derkman let her dance around the room," George reminded Katie.

"And she acted like Rosie was the only one who could do gymnastics," Becky added.

"So be mad at Mrs. Derkman," Katie said.

"Rosie got me fired from her movie," Suzanne remarked.

Katie shook her head. "No, she didn't. You're the one who did all those goofy things. Rosie didn't even say a word."

Suzanne frowned, but she didn't argue with Katie.

Katie looked at her friends. "So we're all in on the plan?" she asked them.

"Okay, Katie Kazoo, you win," George said.

"Great!" Katie exclaimed. She watched the elevator doors. Finally they opened. Rosie, her mother, and Carl all stepped out at once. Mrs. Moran and Carl both looked angry. Rosie just seemed sad.

"Here goes," Jeremy said. He pulled a pad and pencil from his pocket and raced toward Rosie. "Can I have your autograph?" he asked. "You're my favorite star."

"Jeremy?" Rosie asked.

He nodded. "I can't wait for your next movie."

"You'll be waiting a long time," Carl muttered.

Jeremy took his pad and pencil and ran off. Rosie didn't take two steps before George popped up in front of her.

"Hey, Rosie, remember me?" he asked.

Rosie nodded.

"Do you know when *The Kids Are in Charge* is coming out? I'm thinking of taking some friends to see it for my birthday."

"Well, I don't know if . . ." Rosie began.

"You'll be an old man before I work on that movie again," Carl told George.

"I'm not going to the movie because of you," George said. "As long as Rosie's in it I'll be there."

Carl turned white. His face got all scrunched up. George had really made him mad!

"I'm outta here!" George said as he dashed out of Carl's way.

Rosie, Carl, and Mrs. Moran walked out of the lobby. A big black limo was waiting for them. But before they could get in the car, four girls rushed straight for Rosie.

"Wait, don't go!" Becky cried out. "I never got your autograph."

"Me, neither," Suzanne said. "And I really want it for my scrapbook."

Mandy and Miriam held out their autograph books as well.

Rosie didn't know what to say.

Just then, Katie pushed her way through the crowd of girls. "Boy, you've got so many fans," she told Rosie. "Any movie you make will earn a lot of money."

That got Carl's attention.

"I think it's so brave of you not to want to do *this* movie," Katie said.

Rosie looked at her strangely. "I don't?" she asked.

"Of course you don't," Katie continued. "I mean, it's such a silly script. Isn't that what you told me yesterday?"

Rosie had no idea what Katie was talking about. "I guess," Rosie murmured. "I mean I don't know. I don't really remember a lot about yesterday."

"You don't remember ruining my film?" Carl demanded.

"It's *Rosie's* film," Katie reminded him. "That's why she didn't want to say the stupid words in the script. No kid talks like that."

Carl stared at Rosie. "You don't think the

script is good enough?" he asked.

Rosie gulped. "Well . . . I . . . um . . ."

"Rosie's really smart," Katie interrupted. "You should take her advice and get that script rewritten."

"Hmmm," Carl said. "Let me talk to the studio about this."

As Rosie got into the limo, she looked strangely at Katie. Rosie wasn't quite sure what had just happened. All she knew was that Katie had tried to help her.

That was the kind of thing a real friend would do.

Chapter 13

"Katie, the phone's for you!" Mrs. Carew shouted.

Katie came bounding down the stairs. "Who is it?" she asked her mother.

"Rosie Moran," Mrs. Carew answered. "She's calling from Los Angeles."

Katie was surprised. It had been a month since Rosie had gone back to California. Katie hadn't expected to ever hear from her again.

"Hello," Katie said into the phone.

"Hi, Katie Kazoo!" Rosie answered. "I have great news, and I wanted you to be the first one to know."

"What's up?"

"They're going to rewrite *The Kids Are in Charge*. But it's going to be six months before we can start filming again."

"What are you doing until then?" Katie asked.

"I have to reshoot *The Kids Are in Charge* before I can make another movie. So my mom said I could go to a regular school while we wait!"

"And now you'll have lots of time to make friends," Katie said.

"I hope so," Rosie said. "My mom says from now on I can spend more time with kids my own age. She'll figure out a way for me to work and be more like a regular kid, too."

"That's great!" Katie exclaimed.

"It's all because of you," Rosie admitted. "I'm not sure why you wanted to help me. But I'm glad you did."

Katie didn't know what to say. She couldn't tell Rosie that she'd felt really bad about messing up her career. Rosie would never understand about the magic wind.

"I just wanted to help," she said finally.

The girls talked for a little longer. They exchanged e-mail addresses and promised to write. Katie was very excited. She had a movie star for a pen pal!

As she hung up the phone, Katie felt a cool breeze on the back of her neck. She gulped nervously. Was the magic wind back?

"Katie, please shut the kitchen window," her mother called from the other room. "I think we're going to have a storm."

Katie sighed with relief. It was a regular, everyday wind. She would stay herself . . .

At least for now.

Chapter 14

Tough Tongue Twisters

Actors and actresses learn to speak clearly by saying tongue twisters. Here are some of Rosie Moran's favorites. Can you say each one three times, fast?

Four funny farmers found farming far from fun.

Eight gray geese in a green field grazing.

Six silly sailors set sail on the seven seas.

A glad batch of lads catching crabs.

Six thick thistle sticks.